D0496450

This Walker book belongs to:

_____

_____

_____

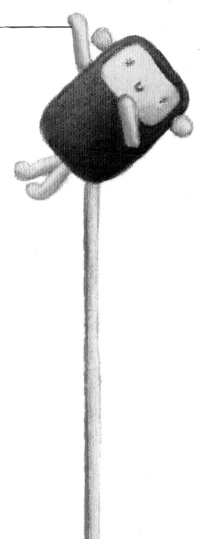

To my brother, John – D.L.

First published 2008 by Walker Books Ltd, 87 Vauxhall Walk, London SE11 5HJ

This edition published 2009

2 4 6 8 10 9 7 5 3 1

This book has been typeset in Memphis

Printed in China

British Library Cataloguing in Publication Data:
a catalogue record for this book is available from the British Library

ISBN 978-1-4063-1958-3

www.walker.co.uk

WALKER BOOKS
AND SUBSIDIARIES
LONDON · BOSTON · SYDNEY · AUCKLAND

Peanut

David Lucas

In the night,
on a tree,
a flower grew.

As the sun rose, the flower opened.

Inside was a monkey, a monkey as big as a pea.

In the warm sun he soon turned golden brown
and grew as big as a nut.

Then …

POP... POP...

his two eyes opened wide.

"How pleasant to be a little peanut,"
said the tiny monkey.
(He didn't really know *what* he was.)
"But I haven't got a name," he said.
"I know, *Peanut!*"

But as the morning turned to afternoon
the flower began to fade and, one by one,
the petals began to fall.
Peanut was astonished.

He looked down.

"The floor
is made
of air!"
he said.

He looked left and right.
"Monsters!" said Peanut.
"Wild animals of every sort.
I'm going to be eaten up!"

The wind blew.
"The tree is
falling over!"
said Peanut.

It began to rain. "The sky is falling down!" said Peanut.

The sun set.
"The sky is on fire!"
said Peanut.
"And now the big light
is going out!"

"It's the End of the World!" said Peanut, and he shut his eyes ...

and waited.

"Excuse me,"
said a voice
in the darkness.
"Can I just
squeeze by?"

"A ghost!" said Peanut.
"I'm being eaten by a ghost!"

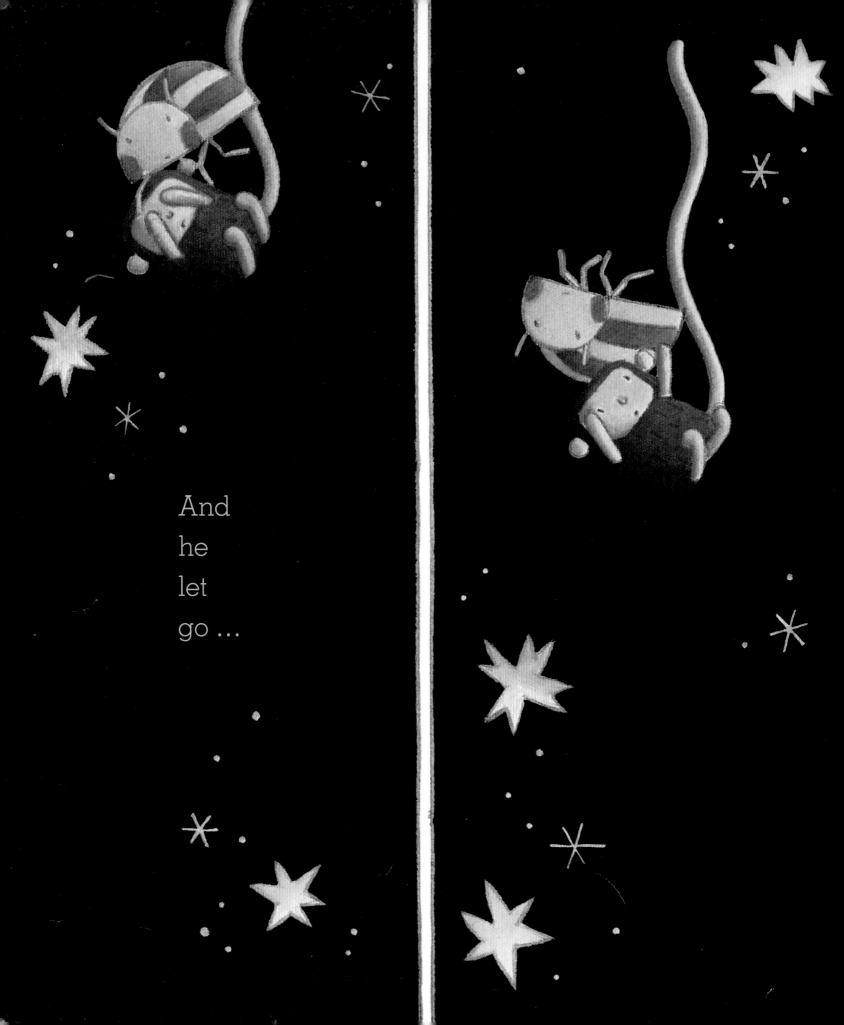

And
he
let
go ...

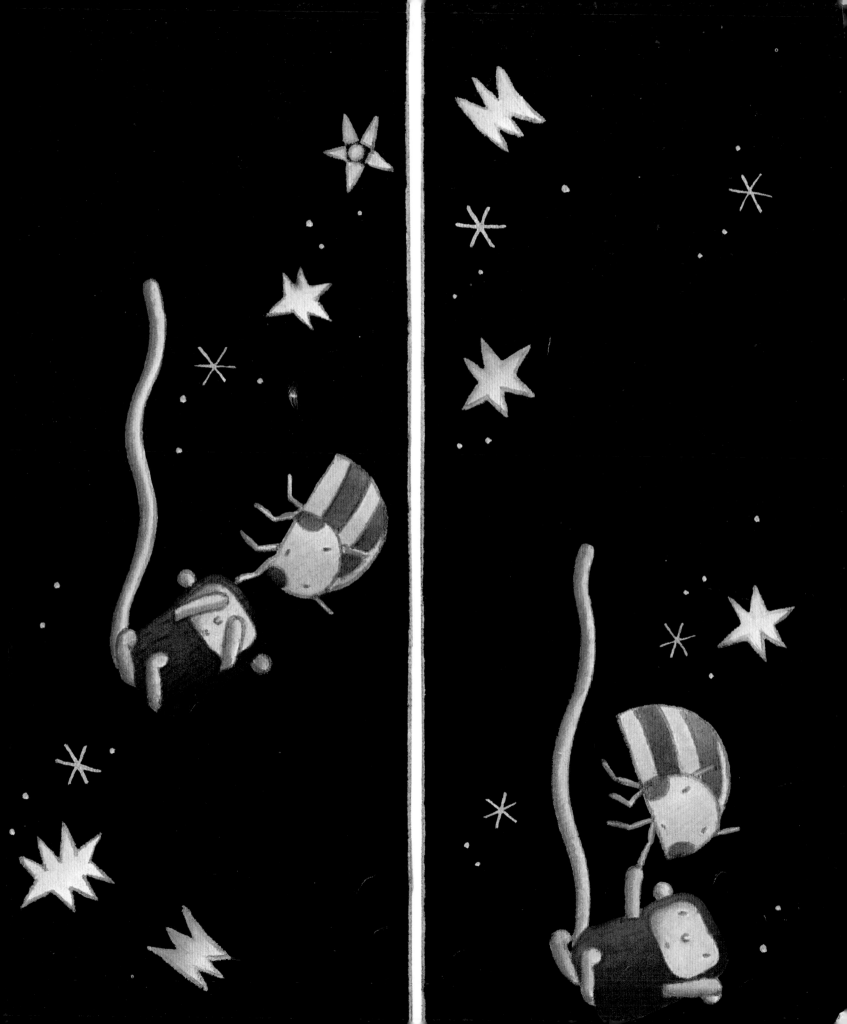

and
caught
another
twig
without
even
thinking.

"Please don't let go!" said the voice.
"A frightened ghost?" said Peanut.
"I'm not a ghost, I'm Beetle."
"Oh," said Peanut. "How do you do?
I'm Peanut. I am a *peanut*."
And he pulled them both up onto the twig.

They sat together
and caught their breath.

"You're not a peanut,
you know," said Beetle.
"You're a monkey."

But Peanut wasn't listening.
"Look," he said.
"The Big Light! Shining bright!"

"It's just another day,"
said Beetle.
"Another one?"
said Peanut.
He hadn't expected *that*.

And that morning
the forest didn't look so frightening at all.
It was a magical forest.
"Come on," said Peanut.
He wanted to explore.
"Yes," said Beetle. "But do let's be careful!"

(actual size)

Peanut
a monkey as big as a nut